A Father's Revenge

Peter G Fitzgerald

GWAA /TSL Publications

First published in Great Britain in 2024
By TSL Publications, Rickmansworth

Copyright © 2024 Peter G Fitzgerald & British South Africa Police Association,
UK Branch

ISBN: 978-1-915660-76-3

Cover courtesy of
P G Fitzgerald

Preface

Peter wrote the skeleton of this book during his convalescence from brain injury. Initially he had no memory and had to be schooled to read and write again. It was a memory test to see how well he was recovering. The book was resurrected following a chance discussion and was expanded to cover not only the African scene but also the return of the principal and his family to the UK. The book draws on Peter's experiences and observations during a difficult period of the lives of both he and his family.

I dedicate this book to my late wife Ann and to my son Craig who have been of tremendous help to me over the years.
Thanks also goes to my sister Geraldine and to my brother Donald who have helped me to complete the second half of this book.

A New Life in Africa

It was a bright, sunny morning and not a cloud in the sky. "This is how summer should be," said Tony Jameson-Brown to himself. Tony was the manager of River Bend mine. In fact, it has been like this for the past four weeks, he thought as he walked down the six steps of his front veranda onto the lush, green grass.

The mine he worked for was a gold mine and got its name from the river which ran at the foot of Tony's front garden. The front of the house looked north across the river. About a mile further on past the house it turned north-west and flowed on its merry way. Although they had not had rain for the past four weeks, the river still had running water, but it was low.

There were two ways to work. The best way was during the dry season, the route he was going to take, was ten minutes quicker. The other way was to walk three hundred yards to the main tar road which went to Johannesburg, turn left, and walk across the high-level bridge, continue for about another three hundred yards to the main mine road.

Tony made his way across the lawn to a small gate. He opened the gate and stepped onto the narrow dirt footpath which ran parallel and down to a crossing point across the river. During that time of the year Tony enjoyed the early mornings. In fact, it was his idea that all the office staff start at 6:00 a.m. during the summer and went off at lunch time. It was a bit hard to accept at first, but the staff soon got used to it and the miners who used to knock off at 7:00 a.m., after a long night, enjoyed seeing people around when they came to the surface. As Tony walked along, he could hear whistling coming from the birds, he looked up into the trees and saw about five distinct types flying from tree to tree. His mind then drifted away to his early days living in the UK and working on the farm.

He was born in England and was the youngest child of four. His eldest brother was a doctor, the second brother ran a chemist, and his sister was a physiotherapist. At that time Tony did not want to be tied down so, in 1953, at the age of seventeen, he joined the British army.

After a few months he managed to pass an interview for the Sandhurst Army College. On arrival at Sandhurst, he met a chap named Vernon Irvin-Brown. He did not team up with this fellow because he had a double-barrelled name, but they appeared to have so much in common and got on well with each other. Tony and Vernon found the going hard at Sandhurst but everything they did they put their heart and soul into. They had so much determination that at night they would sit together and go over the day's activities.

Tony and Vernon's arduous work did not go unrewarded. When pass out day came, they were both placed in high positions. Tony won the sword of honour and Vernon, according to the teachers of the training staff, came a close second. Tony was transferred to a regiment in London and Vernon to one in Manchester. Both were pleased with their posting but sad to see each other go their separate ways.

Tony remained in the army until early January 1956, then went on discharge at his own request. He wrote to Vernon telling him that he was fed up with all the red tape and wanted to see the world. He told him not to answer the letter because he would be out of the army within a few days. He mentioned that he was going to head for a place called Southern Rhodesia via South Africa.

By the end of two weeks, after his army discharge, he wished all his family, relatives and friends goodbye and headed off for Southampton docks where he boarded a ship.

He remembered the journey well, the ship was full of women, and he enjoyed the best three weeks of his life. On approaching Cape Town, South Africa, he saw a large mountain and soon found out that this was the well-known "Table Mountain."

After they had docked, he headed towards the railway station and confirmed his booking to Rhodesia. To his surprise and pleasure, he found out that two of the ladies from the ship were heading for Southern Rhodesia.

His destination was Salisbury, the capital of Southern Rhodesia. On reaching Salisbury he caught a taxi and headed for one of the hotels.

The following morning at about 6:30 a.m. he read the local newspaper *Rhodesia Herald* for farm jobs. He came across one which was about 125 miles out of Salisbury on the main road to Northern Rhodesia, the farm needed an Assistant Manager. He knew that farmers got up early, so he took a chance and phoned the farm. Tony managed to get hold of the owner straight away who told him that his name was Doug Jameson, he also informed Tony that he was coming into Salisbury the following day with his wife and suggested that he meet him at 9:00 a.m. at the hotel at which he was staying.

Life on a Farm

The next day Tony met Doug Jameson and his wife. They were an elderly couple and were genuinely nice. Tony sat with Doug for about an hour and by 2:00 p.m. was heading back to the farm with them. It was not until 5:45 p.m. that they arrived at the farm and Tony was introduced to the manager Robert Clark. He was shown to his own cabin and managed to get settled in. The following morning, he was to report by 5:30 a.m.

That is how Tony's life started in Rhodesia. He enjoyed the farm life and saw many wild animals, such as buck, monkeys, baboons, and leopards to mention but a few. After working for two weeks, he had his first weekend off. Robert Clark took him down to the local club and there he met a few farmers.

He enjoyed the club and right from the word go he got on well with the other farmers. There were several games he could play besides cricket and tennis, which appeared to be the main events. Later that afternoon, whilst at the club, he met Rod McDougal, his wife, and their daughter Sally. Tony liked what he saw and most of the afternoon he and Sally were together.

Sally was only a year younger than Tony. She used to come home every second weekend, but once things started to get a little serious, Sally managed to get home every weekend. Within seven months Tony was given an offer, which he accepted without hesitation. He was made manager of the farm which was approximately 15'000 acres. Life was a lot easier and as far as his love life was concerned, he and Sally were married by January of the following year.

The reception was held at the McDougal's farm and was well patronised by the farmers of the district. During the evening McDougal pulled Tony to one side, and with a Scots accent said to him, "my boy you are the first person to get anything for nothing from me, so you had better manage the subject in question with care and treat it well. In addition to those remarks, for a wedding present, I am going to give you 5'000 acres." Tony was shattered, and it took him a good thirty seconds to speak. "Thank you, Sir," he managed to blurt out. "As far as Sally is concerned, you and Mrs McDougal will have nothing to worry about." "It is not Sally I am worried about, my boy," said McDougal, "it is those 5'000 acres I am going to give you. Tomorrow they are yours, so you had better get out there and earn some money. I have given you enough, so from now on you are on your own."

Tony and Sally stayed with her parents until their house was built. They could not move quick enough. Tony grew tobacco and maize and as soon as he moved onto the farm, he started to build up a herd of Hereford cattle. He struck gold on the farm. It was a small mine he built up and used to work there twice a week. He employed three Africans who worked full time on the mine.

Within three months of their marriage, Sally informed Tony that she was expecting their first child. That set Tony back a little, he did not know whether to be happy or annoyed. Their arrangement was to wait at least a year before starting a family. Sally looked at Tony and said, "well, are you happy or not?" Tony was between the devil and the deep blue sea and said the first thing that came to his mind, "I know who will be happy." "So do I," said Sally, "but I didn't ask them, I asked you." "Of course, I am happy," said Tony, "it just came as a surprise, that's all."

By the end of January 1958, Sally gave birth to a healthy boy. Tony was an incredibly happy father and bought everyone a drink that evening down at the club. Everyone at the club had been through this type of joy themselves, so they knew just how Tony felt.

The baby was named Angus after Sally's grandfather who still lived in Scotland. A year later another boy was born, he was named Craig. A further year on and the battle was won, Sally finally gave birth to a little girl. They named her Alice. This name came about because Tony called his farm "Wonderland." They had many happy days on the farm. The children each had a dog and everywhere they went on the farm, their dogs would follow.

Life was good on the farm until about 1971, then a group of

terrorists killed three of his cows and abducted one of his employees' daughters. According to his employees, the group consisted of twelve men led by a very tall man who was known as Brother John by all his men. The army and police were called in to investigate. Tony was very cross but not half as cross as the next attack.

Within three months the terrorists were back. This time they killed the three Africans who worked on the mine, killed twelve of his cattle and three of his employees and their wives, fired on the house and abducted ten African children. Tony walked down to the kraal to see his staff. It was a very pitiful sight to see, women and children were sitting together in a circle and crying. All the men were standing together at the end of the kraal. Tony approached them and spoke. He was told that it was the same group as before, led by Brother John.

Once again, the army and police were called out. Tony knew the two police officers who arrived. The man in charge of the army was a major and he introduced himself as Alan Bicks. That evening Sally spoke to Tony. "Dear," she said, "as much as I hate to say this, for the children's sake and the staff, we will have to leave the farm. You and I could go it alone, but we have other people to think about."

Tony, who was sitting in a chair, looked up at his wife who was standing in front of him, "yes, my dear, I agree with you, we had better take potluck and move down to South Africa. I think I will be able to manage life a lot better down there rather than here if one of you four get killed." "What about you?" said Sally, "these children are no good without a father and I'm no good without a husband."

Tony's luck held out and he managed to sell the farm within two months, and they all moved down to South Africa. They were all sad to leave the farm but as Tony said, "what must be, must be."

River Bend Mine

Tony looked for a job, but this time his luck was not in. He walked the streets of Johannesburg from 6:00 a.m. till late in the afternoon. He did this for two weeks without success.

One day, during his normal job finding hunt, he bumped into a chap who was walking out of a shop. Tony had his head down and when he looked up, he noticed the person he had bumped into, it was his old friend from Sandhurst, Vernon Irvin-Brown. "Well, this is a surprise," said Tony, "what are you doing in this part of the world, but before you answer that, how are you?" "I'm keeping well," said Vernon, "and you?" "Very well," said Tony. "The last time I heard of you," said Vernon, "was that you were farming somewhere in Rhodesia."

They spoke about the old days, both men were pleased to see each other and could have talked all day, but after about an hour, Vernon said he would have to leave, and he gave Tony one of his cards and asked him to pop in and see him the following day. Tony agreed and went home, pleased to have seen Vernon but a little upset in not finding a job. The time was about 3:00 p.m. and he was fed up with job hunting, so he decided to call it a day.

The following day, at about 10:00 a.m., he paid Vernon a visit. "I'm glad you have come in early," said Vernon. "I have a job for you, if you are interested?" "I'm interested," said Tony. "Knowing you, I thought you would be," said Vernon. "It's a mine managers job." "What the hell do I know about mining," said Tony. "Very little I suppose," said Vernon, "but you have had your own small mine, so you know what gold is all about, in addition, you are a hardworking man who has plenty of courage and tact."

That is how Tony started at River Bend mine, and has been there ever since, eight years he thought. His mind then drifted to Angus. I wonder what that little devil is up to, we have not heard from him for a good month. Tony remembered July 1978, Angus was having a beer on the back veranda with him, when he said, "Dad, I want to have a chat with you." He then walked down the steps of the veranda onto the lawn. Tony followed him, and in a joking type of voice said, "this must be a serious chat." "It is," said Angus. He stopped and turned around, he looked Tony straight in the eyes and said, "Dad, I want to join the army." Tony, who was in good humour, looked at Angus and said, "a chip off the old block, hey." "I want to become an officer like you were." "Well son I don't mind, we will miss you, but Pretoria isn't very far away." "Dad," said Angus, "I have not explained myself very well. I am a Rhodesian as you know, and I want to fight for them." "What about your job at the bank?" said Tony. "I have given in my notice and on Monday next week the first Board of Officers will be held, and I want to be at that board." Just then Sally appeared on the top veranda step and shouted out "is it a men-only chat or can women attend?" "Yes, you can attend," said Tony. Sally walked up to them, and Angus looked straight at her, "I have left the bank, Mum. I want to join the army," said Angus. "He hasn't told you which army," said Tony. Sally looked back at Angus and said, "which army?" "The Rhodesian, Mum," said Angus. "Well it's a good army my son," said Sally, "but you are not twenty-one years old yet and both your father and I could stop you, but as your twenty-first birthday is only months away, I cannot see any point in stopping you, can you Dad?" "No," said Tony, "we don't like the idea, but we will not stop you." "Thank you," said Angus. Three days later they were at Jan Smuts airport to see him off on the 4:00 p.m. flight to Salisbury. Sally had tears in her eyes, the other two children were at university.

That was the last time they saw him. His thoughts were interrupted as he looked down at the river. The path ran close to the river at this point and was approximately ten feet higher. He saw some of the bushes in the river move. In thought, he said to himself: "I wonder if it is that crocodile." This crocodile had been seen by some of the local farmers who said it was about ten feet long. It had taken one of John Naude's cows about three weeks ago, the incident occurred on his farm three miles away.

Tony then saw two Leguaans (this is the largest of African lizards and will grow up to 2.5 metres. It looks like a crocodile in shape, with a serpent-like head, longish legs, and strong hooked claws). There are two varieties of Leguaans that Tony knew of. The rock and water type, it was the water type he saw. "Ha," he said aloud, "now I know who is eating my chickens." They were approximately twelve feet in front of him. Tony did not know what sex they were, he just saw one chasing the other, they ran across the path in front of him and into the bush.

He then stopped thinking of his past and quickened his pace down to the river. The river was extremely low and moving slowly along. There were ten large rocks across the river, about eighteen inches apart and were sticking out of the water. Tony then thought, before I run into any more Leguaans or that big croc, I had better get across this river. He jumped from rock to rock and ran up the path to the other side. He stopped and looked around; he saw nothing except the river moving along at its slow speed. Tony was in his early forties and was very fit for his age, in fact, he looked more like a man in his thirties.

He then turned around and saw the mine and office approximately five hundred metres away, he increased his speed a little bit towards the mine office, it was nearly 6:00 a.m. As he moved along, he saw two of his African employees, John and Cecil, emptying dirt into a large hole. He called out to them, "good morning, is everything alright?" They returned his greeting and informed him that all was well, at least their day has started off well, thought Tony.

As Tony got nearer to the mine office, he saw old man Richards. He used to be a miner but had now retired, and worked at the mine as a handyman. Jean Naude, one of the typists, was talking to him and Peter Du Plessis was standing with them. On the other side of the veranda steps stood Alan Smit the pay clerk and Clive Van Rensberg one of the engineers.

Tony greeted them all and proceeded up the front steps to unlock the large double oak doors, everyone followed him into the building and branched off to their offices. Tony's office was the last one along the passage. As he placed the key in the lock, he heard someone running up behind him, it was his secretary, Laura Stofberg.

Laura was born in Wales. At the age of two she immigrated to Southern Rhodesia with her parents and went to Wankie where her father worked on the mine. At the age of seventeen, she went with her parents to South Africa. Her father Mr John had made the move because it meant more money. At the age of twenty-two she met and married her husband, she was now thirty years old and had two children, a little boy and girl.

"Well how are things treating you, Laura?" "Not too bad Mr Jameson-Brown, but I shall be glad when Jeff is off night shift." "That reminds me, Laura, would you please call me at 6:50 a.m., just before the night shift ends?" "Certainly," she said. He then went on to his own office which led off at the rear side of her office. It was large and had two big windows which were covered with venetian blinds and red sun filter curtains.

Tony enjoyed being at work early because between 6 and 7 a.m. he could get some of his work up to date, see the night shift when it went off and the day shift when it came on, then pop off to breakfast between 7 and 8 a.m. before that dreaded telephone started ringing, this of course was the main reason, but there were several others. His office was in its usual neat condition, he walked to the windows, opened them, thought to himself, "today will be another scorcher."

He sat down, opened his top right-hand drawer, and took out some letters. He managed to get through quite a lot of work, then Laura came in and told him it was 6:50 a.m. He gave a low whistle and said, "so soon, you know it only seems half an hour since we walked into the office, time flies for us but for those chaps down the mine, I bet it drags." "It does," said Laura.

She is a good worker, thought Tony. There is not much you can tell her about a mine, she has lived on them all her life. "Bye for now, I shall see you at 8:00 a.m.," said Tony. "Don't forget to send my husband over here," shouted Laura as he went through the front door, "otherwise he walks home."

Tony walked out of the office and down to the mine. He could see several men standing around talking just above the shaft which takes them underground. Approaching, Tony greeted them good morning and the reply was returned by all. Tony stopped and joined them as he normally did, the topic of conversation was rugby. Some of the chaps said Northern Transvaal would beat the World 15, whereas others said the score would be close, but the World 15 would win. "Do not take your argument underground fellows, I want some gold dug out today." They all laughed as the first shift of mine workers came up to the surface.

"Well, it is all yours," said one of the night shift men, as the first bunch of morning shift men entered the lift to take them underground. When the second lot of men came up, he saw Jeff Stofberg, they greeted each other, then Tony told Jeff that he had better go across to Laura, otherwise he would have to walk home. Jeff lowered his head and smiled as he shook it, a large peel of laughter came from his work mates. "Never mind Jeff, I will give you a lift home and tuck you into bed," the laughter grew louder. Jeff knew who had said that. He looked up and saw Ivan Smit smiling. "The last time you gave me a lift home I was three hours late, drunk and had to go without a dinner." More laughter was heard and even Tony joined in. "My friend," Jeff said, "I shall take my chances with the old woman, she is more dependable, trustworthy and knows how to tuck me into bed." He then headed off amongst laughter towards the office block where Laura waited.

After all the men from the night shift had come to the surface and the morning shift had replaced them, Tony left for home. He went back the same way he had come. On reaching home he was met by Sally and a set breakfast of bacon and eggs. He returned to work by 8:00 a.m. and on entering the office, the telephone rang. "Here we go," thought Tony. It was head office in Johannesburg. Tony knew the voice, it was Vernon. "You are early for a city dweller," Tony said. Vernon laughed, "I am just checking on you district types." Tony knew that he was not and that the phone call was strictly business.

Tony received very few phone calls that morning and as a result, managed to get through a large amount of work. At about 12:50 p.m. his phone rang, "that is odd," thought Tony. "I very seldom get any calls at this time of the day, anyway, there is a first time for everything." He picked up the telephone, "Hallo, Jameson-Brown speaking." On the other end he heard Sally's voice, she was crying, and he heard the name of his eldest son, Angus, the rest he could not understand because Sally was so upset. "Hold on a few minutes and I shall come straight home, I cannot understand what you are saying." He then put the phone down. Tony realised there was something wrong.

He put his coat on and rushed out of the office. Laura looked at him as he rushed past her and through the office. Something must be wrong. I have never seen him move that fast before. "Appears to be a problem at home, Laura. I shall see you later this afternoon or tomorrow," said Tony. He ran all the way home, whether the crocodile was waiting for him at the river or not, it would not have caught him, it would have been surprised at the speed a human could move.

When Tony got home, Craig and Alice were standing by the steps on the veranda. Craig had his right arm around Alice, who looked full of tears. Still crying, Sally then went to stand in the middle of the lawn. A thought quickly went through his mind, "the last time we stood on that spot was when Angus told us he was going to join the Rhodesian army." He walked straight up to Sally, "whatever is wrong, my dear?" She looked up at him, "Angus has been killed by terrorists." Tony looked at Sally for about fifteen seconds before it sank in. Tears came to his eyes, and he said, "my God not Angus."

Tony put his arm around Sally, and they walked into the house. Craig and Alice followed them into the lounge. "How did you two find out?" said Tony to his son and daughter. "We managed to catch a lift, Dad," said Craig, and the telegram arrived as we walked through the door. Sally and the children had never seen Tony so cross or swear. Tony leapt up and said, "I am going to Rhodesia, and I am going to find the bastard who killed Angus and kill him."

None of the family agreed with Tony going to Rhodesia, but Sally knew he would do what he thought was best. After calming everyone down, Tony walked slowly back to work. Laura, his secretary, was still there when he arrived. "What are you doing here, my girl?" said Tony. "Just catching up on some work," replied Laura. "You certainly do not look as fresh as you were early this morning. Is there a problem, or have you had some unwelcome news?" she asked. Tony looked up at her, "do you remember my son Angus?" "Very well," said Laura. "Well, he has been killed by terrorists whilst fighting for the Rhodesian army."

"My God," said Laura. She put both her hands to her mouth and said, "you must excuse me for the rest of the afternoon Mr Jameson-Brown." "I will," said Tony. She picked up her handbag and quickly left the room.

Tony walked into his office slowly and closed the door. He turned his chair away from his desk to the right and looked out of the window. He told his wife that he would not be long at the office, he just wanted to see that everything was all right and telephone Vernon at head office. He managed to get through to Vernon straight away. "Afternoon," said Tony. "My, this is a pleasant surprise," said Vernon. "You are often away by this time of the day, is there something wrong?" Tony remained silent for a few seconds, then said, "there is Vernon, but it has nothing to do with the mine." "You certainly want to speak about something, old friend, what has happened?" said Vernon. Do you remember my son Angus?" said Tony. "Very well," replied Vernon. "He went to Rhodesia and joined the army." "Yes," replied Tony. "Well, we have just received a telegram from Rhodesia informing us that he has been killed." "My goodness," said Vernon "how did this happen?" "He was shot," replied Tony. "In view of this, I want to resign and see if I can join the Rhodesian army."

"Before we go any further, Tony," said Vernon, "please accept my condolences and those of my family." "Thank you, Vernon," said Tony. "I do not want to lose you, Tony, under different circumstances I would try and talk you out of leaving, in fact, putting the present to one side for a minute, I will be very sad to see you go, but knowing you and the type of person you are, I cannot stand in your way, and if you ever return, and I am still here, you will have a job to come back to." "Thank you," said Tony, "not only are you a true and honest boss, but a fine friend as well."

Within three days Tony and his family went up to Salisbury to attend Angus' funeral. Tony stayed behind in Salisbury, against the wishes of the family, who flew back to Johannesburg. Everything had been rush-rush, but with Vernon's help they managed to get a flat for Sally and the two children when they were on holiday from varsity. Once the family had left, Tony booked in at one of the hotels which brought back old memories.

Back to the Army

The next day he reported to the army headquarters at about 10:00 a.m. and went before three officers. Although he was just over forty-three, his fitness and good health made him look like he was in his mid-thirties. The fact that he had been to Sandhurst and lived in Rhodesia, swung the verdict in his favour. The following day he reported to a particular barracks just outside of Salisbury. The barracks were under the command of Colonel Alan Bicks. After reporting to the guard room at about 7:50 a.m., he was told that Colonel Bicks wanted to see him. On arriving at the Commanding Officer's (C.O.) office whom he first saw and reported to, a lieutenant, who went into a nearby office, came back after a few seconds and said, "the C.O. will see you now." "Thank you, Sir," said Tony.

As Tony walked into the office, he saw the C.O. seated at a desk and a large window with blue curtains behind him. He looked at the Colonel and thought, "I've seen you before old chap, but I'll be damned if I can remember where or when." The Colonel rose and said, "good morning, Mr Jameson-Brown, welcome to Rhodesia and the barracks. Do you remember me?" "I, good morning, Sir, I do remember you, but I cannot place you, Sir." The Colonel smiled and said, "I shall refresh your memory, can you remember when the terrorist raided your farm for the second time?" "Do not say any more, Sir, it has come to me, you were a Major at the time, and you introduced yourself." "Correct," said the Colonel." "Well, it is nice to see you again, Sir," said Tony, "of course the circumstances are a little different." "Yes, they are," said the Colonel.

"Anyway, Tony, you do not mind me calling you by your Christian name?" "Not at all, Sir," said Tony. "Good," said the Colonel, "take a seat and I shall tell you what I have worked out for you." They both sat down, and the Colonel went straight into business. "Tony, I am giving you a sergeants rank to start with, then in three months' time, I am sending you on an Officers' course."

Tony spent the three months in the headquarters office and learnt how everything worked. After this he went to the Officers Training School. To his surprise he knew more than he thought. After he passed out, he was given ten days off, so he flew down to Johannesburg and surprised his family. On the tenth day he flew back to Salisbury and reported to the C.O.

He was informed by the C.O. that he would stay at headquarters for about a month, then he would be transferred to one of the units. After a month he was transferred to "A" company. He remained with "A" company for three months. After about five contacts with terrorists, he was called to the C.O.'s office.

Tony arrived at the C.O.'s office at 9:00 a.m., the arranged time he had set to meet him. He went straight into his office without waiting. "Good morning, Tony," said the Colonel, "please be seated." "Good morning, Sir," said Tony, saluted then sat down. "Well Tony, I am very satisfied with you. At the end of this month Major Bell is retiring and will be leaving the Johnny Alsorts company. You will take over that company on the day he leaves and on the same date, you will be promoted to Captain, so in the meantime, you remain with 'A' company. There is only one hitch to this promotion, and taking over your own company," said the Colonel. "There always is Sir," said Tony with a smile on his face. "Yes," said the Colonel. "I'm sorry to tell you this Tony, but the day you take over the company, you will be going straight out to the bush."

"You are taking over a good company Tony. I will want to see you before you leave. That is all for the time being," said the Colonel. Tony stood up, saluted, and said "thank you Sir," about turned and marched out of the office. Once outside Tony walked over to the "A" company office. He wanted to go over to the Johnny Alsorts company, but he thought he had better not. "Let the chap enjoy his last few days in the army," thought Tony.

This went quickly and the day to take over the Johnny Alsorts company soon came around. Tony was putting some papers together when he heard a knock on the door, he opened it, and standing outside were two lieutenants. They both saluted Tony. The one lieutenant introduced them both. "Sir, we are both from the Johnny Alsorts company. I am Lieutenant Brice, and this is Lieutenant Ndhlovu. We will accompany you over to your new quarters, Sir, and carry some of your luggage, also introduce you to the rest of the company." "Thank you, chaps," said Tony, "come inside, close the door, and sit down. I want to speak to you both before I meet the company." The two lieutenants found a couple of chairs. Tony sat on the end of the bed. Tony looked at Lieutenant Brice and said, "what is your Christian name Lieutenant?" "Allan, Sir." "And yours Lieutenant Ndhlovu?" "Simon, Sir." I am sure you know my surname, if not, it is Jameson-Brown, but my Christian name is Tony. When we are together and alone, let us address one another by first names, although being the senior detail, I will call you by your first names, even when the troops are around, unless there is another senior officer present." "Well, chaps, let us get over to my new quarters, see the C.O., then get this show on the road." Simon then said, "the company would like to see you, Tony, before they go out, they are all on the parade ground."

Tony arranged his new quarters and saw the C.O. before he went to see his men. When he arrived at the parade ground with both his lieutenants, he at once understood what they meant by the name Johnny Alsorts company. It had been made up of Europeans, Africans, Coloureds, Indians, and Chinese. Even the ranks from lance corporal to sergeant major were made up of these men. They were really "B" company and had won the most medals in battle. This was the company Angus was in when he got killed. He felt proud as he looked at them. "I will revenge Angus' death with the help of these men," he said to himself.

Tony started off by saying, "good morning, chaps. I am sorry I must meet you on the parade square, and that we are going out to the operational area within a few hours of me taking over the company. I will need your help; in fact, I will always need your assistance. What I do not need is fooling around and lack of discipline. I have heard that you are a good company, but I shall find out for myself." He turned around to his two lieutenants and said, "check the men, see that they have all their equipment, then put them in the trucks."

The company set off in their vehicles at about 8:30 a.m., they travelled for about three hours on the road which led to Zambia, then turned off onto a dirt road which was on their left. After about an hour, they stopped and were made up of two platoons, then sent into the bush to guard the men who were making the camp. After the camp was complete, a platoon, under a coloured sergeant, was sent out to patrol a two-mile radius around the camp.

Tony arranged a meeting with his two lieutenants, sergeant major, sergeants, and corporals for 7 p.m. that evening. Tony greeted the men by saying, "good evening, gentlemen. You know that a new broom sweeps clean. This is one point I have in mind; the other point is in connection with this meeting. It is getting to know you, and we shall hold it every Friday at this time. We must all know what is going on."

"Well, gentlemen, I know the two lieutenants, the sergeant major and Sergeant Bailey. So, from the left side of the table, round to the right, please give me your full names, do not bother about your rank, I can see that." All the men gave Tony their full names. "Mine is Jameson-Brown," said Tony. "I received no instructions about this company or briefing about this area. I will have to go on what you tell me, because I believe you have been here before." "That is correct," said Lieutenant Ndhlovu.

"I believe, according to old reports, you used to send a squad of ten men out and ten areas were covered, is that correct?" "Yes, Sir," said several sergeants seated together. "What would you all say if we cut the squads down to five men, bring the corporals in so that they have their own squad, reduce the patrol area in size so that it can be patrolled quicker, and if it is attacked or it sees the enemy run into someone else's area, it can follow them and advise the patrol in that area that they are getting visitors and set up ambush positions on their borders? The men in charge will be the detail who are to oversee the squad who first saw the enemy, irrespective of his rank, until or unless he is joined by an officer. Remember, once contact is made, you will all be in danger from flying bullets. I cannot tell you anymore, because I do not know how the situation will develop and each one will be different."

"Remember, you must not make contact, unless the enemy is right on top of you or the detail in command gives you an order. You will all have radios, so always stay connected with each other, especially when you are on the border of another area section, I do not want you shooting each other." He looked around and saw everyone smiling, Lieutenant Ndhlovu was the first to speak. "We all agree to this, Sir. This is something we have been after for a long time." "All agree?" said Tony. He then heard an enormous "yes" as everyone put up their hands.

The following day five men of twenty sections went out on patrol. One section was making its way past a small dam, when an African woman called out that her small son was drowning. The corporal in charge, Corporal Moyo and one of the privates, Private Simmons, left the other three in the bush whilst they ran to this woman. When they were about ten feet away from her and in the open, a terrorist on the other side of the dam opened fire on them. The corporal was shot in the head and died straight away, the private was shot in the legs and managed to crawl behind a small rock and return the fire.

The other three had to move forward out of the bush to some high ground above the dam before they could return the fire. They had been walking south and fired on from the west so by use of the radio, they called the men who were on their west side to come behind the terrorist. Within forty-five minutes the section under Sergeant Van Zyl appeared on the other side of the dam. Van Zyl shouted across the dam, "we have not seen them." "Where the hell could they have gone to," thought Lance Corporal Davies. "Stay there please, Sarg, whilst we get these two out, and contact base camp." "Okay, will do," shouted Van Zyl.

Tony was a bit sad that evening. He was talking to both his lieutenants, "my first time out with the company and I lose a darn good corporal and I get a good private injured. I do not understand that section in the west not seeing them, or the three men who were going south. There is a lot of open ground. Tomorrow, I want to visit that kraal which is nearby. They must be able to tell me something."

The following day Tony went to the kraal, he found nothing out, except the name they called the terrorist headman. It was Brother

John, and he was very tall. He had been in the area for a good few years and everyone feared him, even his own men.

Tony thought of his old farm which was only about eighty miles away and thought of this terrorist they called Brother John. "I wonder if it is the chap who attacked my old farm, which will be a coincidence," thought Tony.

The more Tony thought of this terrorist they called Brother John, the more he believed he was the man who attacked his old farm. Tony took his company back home after six weeks, but this name, Brother John the terrorist, played on his mind. I know who will know him, Colonel Bicks, so I shall go and see him.

The following day, after he had returned, Tony made an appointment to see Colonel Bicks. "Sir," said Tony, "please forgive me but I want to clear up a point which I think you may know in respect to the area I have just come from." "I thought you would make a few enquiries, Tony," said the Colonel. "What is bothering you?" "Well, Sir, my company came across a terrorist leader by the name of Brother John, everyone is afraid of him, including his own men. He is the man who attacked my farm."

"Well, you are right, Tony, he also killed your son. I did not want to tell you before because it was your first patrol with that company. I know that you want to revenge your son's death, but you must not forget about the men in your company. You have already had one killed, no fault of your own, may I add. He will not be your last, so remember, you have a company of men to look after. Anyway, Tony, take your ten days off and forget everything, go, and see your wife and family." "Thank you, Sir," said Tony. "You have eased my mind." He got up, saluted the Colonel, and marched out of the office.

That evening Tony flew back to Johannesburg and was met by his wife and two children. For the next nine days Tony relaxed and both he and his wife, Sally, walked around Johannesburg like tourists. Tony told his family that all was well in Rhodesia, and not as bad as certain people make it out to be. He also told them about the company he commanded, but one thing he did not tell them was that he had found Brother John and that he was responsible for Angus' death.

The Revenge

Tony returned to camp and joined his company. He was on his third patrol when his five men patrols worked out. A bunch of twelve terrorists were caught in an area and surrounded. They were defeated by the Johnny Alsorts within half an hour. The Alsorts received no injuries and were just as happy as Tony, but Brother John was not with them. "It is not Brother John's group, it is another group passing through," thought Tony.

Tony was on his tenth patrol with the Johnny Alsorts when they caught another bunch of terrorists, fifteen in number, and wiped them all out within half an hour. All the men were pleased and so was Tony. He was happy in respect of three points, they were: his five men patrols were working, none of his men were injured and they won their battle. Even the men who were not involved in the contact were happy.

On the twelfth patrol he had a sergeant, lance corporal and a private killed near the dam. Once again it was the same circumstances as Tony's first patrol to the area. This was the only incident which occurred in the whole of that area whilst they were there. Tony thought he would resign whilst the going was good.

When he got back to the barracks, the first thing he did after seeing that his men were being looked after, was submit his discharge. I will be sorry to leave these lads and not avenge Angus, but my family needs me. I must give thought to the living. I have one more patrol to do with these good men, "who knows," said Tony to himself. "I may be lucky; I have one thing in mind."

On the second last day of his patrol, Tony called the two lieutenants, plus two sergeants, and two corporals together. It was about 8:00 p.m. when he called them to his quarters. "Hallo chaps," Tony said when they had all arrived. "I am still thinking of this terrorist leader Brother John, tomorrow is our last day before we go home, and Brother John has not shown himself. I have come to one conclusion, so therefore, I am going to take a chance and gamble on it."

"Tomorrow we shall all go out together. When we are about a mile from the dam, Lieutenant Ndhlovu and Sergeant Van Zyl will branch off to the left, with Sergeant Van Zyl walking slightly ahead of Lieutenant Ndhlovu. Lieutenant Ndhlovu in the open, but behind the high-level section which runs parallel to the dam, and on the odd occasion his men will show themselves for a few seconds."

"I, Lieutenant Brice, Sergeant Pepper, Corporals Ching Wong and Khumalo will walk in the bush down the west side. Since we have not seen them, they have an underground passage, which is well camouflaged. It is the only idea I can come up with, because just now I think he will move out. We have not heard about him for a long time, so I hope he has not gone already."

They moved out the next morning, about 7:00 a.m., approximately thirty men under Tony's command. When they were about a mile from the dam, they split up. Tony went along the west side, heading south, and Lieutenant Ndhlovu walked on the east side going south. On reaching the dam, Tony's men walked out in straight lines, it was a small dam and Tony could see Lieutenant Ndhlovu's men pop into view on the odd occasion. Tony heard the African woman shout out for help, he looked across the dam and saw her. Suddenly he heard the man next to him fire, it was Sergeant Pepper, it was a terrorist who had moved only two feet in front of him.

"The game is on now," thought Tony. They had walked right into the terrorist without them knowing. The men who were on the right turned left and added extra fire, everything was over within five minutes. The Johnny Alsorts had won again, without injury or death to a man. Tony then saw a tall man get up and run towards the houses in a nearby kraal. Instinct told Tony who this man was, Brother John.

With no respect to bullets flying around him, Tony chased after the terrorist leader. Brother John knew that he was being chased. When he was near the houses, he fired at Tony from the hip, but at the same time he tripped backwards over a rock and fell, his shot went high over Tony's head, Brother John was soon on his feet again. Tony gained a yard on him. Brother John knew that the soldier behind him was gaining.

When Brother John was behind two houses, he stopped quickly and turned fast, Tony anticipated this, he jumped over to the right and fired two shots from his waist. One bullet hit Brother John in the chest and the other between the ears. Brother John was straightaway dead. Tony walked up to him and looked down, he then looked up towards the sky and said, "I have avenged you, Angus."

Tony turned around and saw three of his soldiers looking at him smiling, with all the people from the kraal standing behind them smiling too. "Well done, Sir," said one of the three soldiers who was a sergeant. "Thanks, Sergeant," said Tony, "would you please take care of this one," pointing to the deceased Brother John, "call the camp on a radio, ask them to send a truck here, then you three take him back to the camp." "Yes Sir," said the sergeant.

As Tony walked away, he shouted to the sergeant to search him. The sergeant again said, "yes, Sir." As Tony walked past the other houses, in front of him he heard, "well done, Sir." He turned his head around and saw Lieutenant Ndhlovu and Sergeant Van Zyl, both were smiling. "If he had got away from you," said the Lieutenant, "he certainly would not have passed us." "I am sure of that," said Tony, and walked over to them.

Tony had been speaking to the lieutenant and the sergeant for about five minutes when Corporal Ching Wong ran up to him. "Sir," said Ching Wong, "Lieutenant Brice wants to show you something." When Tony reached Brice, he said, "I believe you want to see me, Lieutenant." "Yes Sir," said Brice. "Do you notice anything on the ground here, Sir?" Tony looked at the ground and around the area, "no Lieutenant, I don't."

"Private James," said Brice, "move the top." Once the top had been lifted Tony saw an underground passage which would take the size of a man if he crawled through it. "The crafty buggers," said Tony. "No wonder the men patrolling the west side never saw them, and it is well camouflaged." "Is there anyone in there, Lieutenant?" said Tony. "Sir, we shouted inside three times but got no answer, so we threw in three grenades." "How deep is it?" "About three feet, Sir."

When the company got back to the barracks, Tony was told by a young lieutenant that the C.O. wanted to see him. He told his two lieutenants to see that the men were looked after and then he went over to the C.O.'s office. "Hallo, I am glad to see you and all your men back in one piece, anyway, take a seat. Tony, firstly, let me congratulate you on getting Brother John. Secondly, this hurts me more than you, your discharge has been accepted, so as from twelve midnight you are a civilian again."

After about twenty minutes with the commanding officer, he left the office. He was met outside by his two lieutenants, who said, "Well Sir, it is now our turn, come with us please." They walked towards the parade square, on reaching it he saw all his men on parade. "Okay, Sir, tell them why you are leaving us." Tony looked at both the lieutenants with tears in his eyes. He then turned around to his men and said, "I really do not know what to say to you. This is one occasion when I am lost for words. I must go on discharge because my family needs me. I am deeply sorry to leave you chaps. I was a coward to say goodbye to you, because I like each and every one of you, and in view of that, I was going to just walk out, but I should have known that I could not fool Johnny Alsorts."

"Please, chaps, when you are done here, I will see you all, and I mean all at the common bar. I will leave at 5:00 p.m. to catch the 6:00 p.m. flight to Johannesburg. So, there is a little job like phoning my wife before I see you all in the bar, but before I go, I would like to tell you that I was immensely proud of serving in the same company as my son, the late Lieutenant Angus Jameson-Brown. I know now that he was a member of a good company."

Tony said goodbye to all the men, then was rushed off to the airport by the two lieutenants. On arrival, he bid them both goodbye and walked to the departure lounge. He walked over to the plane and when he was about halfway there, singing broke out to the sound of "he's a jolly good fellow." Tony turned around, and to his surprise, he saw the full Johnny Alsorts company singing and shouting good luck to him.

Tony stood still looking at the men until they finished. He waved to them, turned, and walked to the aircraft. At the top of the steps, before entering the aircraft, he turned around to the men and waved again. The men stood and watched the plane until it flew out of sight. He reached Johannesburg, about an hour later, his wife Sally and his two children, Craig and Alice, were waiting for him. He had yet to tell them that he had left the army or revenged Angus however, by the smile on his face, Sally sensed he was home for good.

Return to the Family

Tony surveyed all the airport hustle and bustle around his family group and could hardly believe that he was once again back with the family he had missed so much during his many months of military service in the bush. Sally was equally as happy to have her husband back home as were daughter, Alice, and son, Craig, to see their father. The family was doubly happy because the reunion was taking place during the university holiday break.

It was late by the time they arrived home from the airport, so Alice just made a little welcome snack for them all and promised to make amends by making a special "welcome home" dinner the following evening. Exhausted and happy, Tony and the family decided that after all the celebrations they would make it a short evening and retire.

The following morning Tony awakened to the sound of Sally calling him to breakfast and suddenly realised that he had slept longer than he had planned. As he made his way along the corridor, a welcome smell of coffee and toast greeted him at the kitchen door. "Good morning, Tony," said Sally. "I see that you slept well, not even the early birds could wake you."

That evening, to celebrate the occasion, Sally decided to make Tony's favourite dish of beef roast with all the trimmings accompanied by a good bottle of South African wine and for the children an alternative fizzy drink.

As the dinner was coming to an end, Tony decided that this was the time to tell the family that he had fulfilled his quest to avenge the death of Angus and was now definitely finished with the army. Craig rose from his chair and putting his hand on his dad's shoulder said, "well done Dad, I'm so proud of you, as we all are." Sally and Alice, with tears in their eyes, joined Tony and Craig so they could all hug one another.

The next day, Tony decided to contact Vernon, his old friend from earlier times. After all Vernon did say that if he needed a job on his return, he should give him a call. He picked up the phone and dialled the familiar number. "Good morning, this is Tony Jameson-Brown speaking." "Well, I'll be," said Vernon Irvin-Brown. "When did you get back from the army?" "The day before yesterday," said Tony. "Everything went to plan, just as I had envisaged it and I have no future desire to serve an army." Vernon told Tony that he was terribly busy at that moment and would only be able to see him the following Thursday. There was a job going at the head office of the mining company and he suggested Tony visit his office at 9:30 a.m. that Thursday.

On the appointed day Tony made his way to Vernon's office at the arranged time but Vernon was nowhere to be seen. As he explored the reception area, he glanced down a corridor where he saw Vernon at the other end having a conversation with a man. Tony slowly walked towards Vernon and as he got closer, he heard Vernon say, "here is Tony Jameson-Brown, the applicant I told you about." Vernon then introduced Tony to his boss Pete Smit, the managing director of the mine company. Vernon went on to say that he had moved office as he had recently been promoted and had taken on another position in the company. Vernon said he did not have much time at the present but would contact Tony as soon as possible. Vernon wished both men an enjoyable day and left them.

The two of them continued their walk down the corridor admiring the photos of various mines that flanked it. They eventually got to Pete's office which he had changed to his own liking. During Vernon's time the office had been light with minimum furniture and not too many ornaments standing about. Vernon would say, "They were dust collectors." Pete had put more colour and pictures in the room, which made it look more inviting and made one feel comfortable.

"Please sit down, Tony. I hope you do not mind me calling you by your Christian name. Please call me Pete." "No," replied Tony "not at all." Pete then got down to business and said, "let us continue with your job interview. I have heard a lot about you from Vernon, from you getting to know one another in the UK to how you got the job at the River Bend mine and your good performance there. Presently, we do not have a mine job for you, but we do have a position here at head office which with your experience, we believe you will fit into very well." Tony thanked Mr Smit and said he would accept the offer and looked forward to receiving the contract.

Tony really enjoyed his new position. He found his previous experience at the mining company allowed him to stay on top of the job which meant he did not have to work late hours like before and was home early enough to enjoy the pleasure of dining with Sally and the children, when they were at home. He did miss being hands-on though.

He was about ten months into his new job when he received a long-awaited call from Pete Smit. "How would you like to take on a mine management position?" asked Pete. "Which mine?" asked Tony. Pete replied, "River Bend mine, I think you are familiar with the work there." Tony did not have to think twice, he wanted the position, but he needed to discuss this with Sally. The children were grown up now, still at university, so they would only come home during the varsity holidays. Sally might find the mine life slow compared with city living.

After discussions with Sally, he then went to see Pete Smit to thank him for this new position which he gladly accepted even though the family were now settled in their suburban home outside of Johannesburg, but Tony was so happy to be returning to a job he loved. To get things going with accommodation, he decided to give his previous secretary, Laura Stofberg a call. "Good afternoon, Laura. This is Tony Jameson-Brown. How are you, Jeff and the family keeping?" "This is a welcome surprise, Mr Jameson-Brown. I did hear through the grapevine that you might be coming back. I was so pleased to hear that. Do hope you have all kept well in the meantime?" "Yes, thank you, Laura. We are all fine, however we would be grateful if you could make the necessary living arrangements before we make the journey to the mine."

The day arrived when Tony and Sally made their way to the River Bend mine. They managed to sort themselves out and get settled in to the familiar surroundings. As was traditional for new management, Laura had arranged for the staff to attend a reception the following evening. Some of the old staff were still there and Tony thought this would be an excellent opportunity to meet everyone again, to meet the new staff and to get feedback on what had been going on during his absence.

Tony was really enjoying his old job again. He would take the usual way to work as he did previously. The gate at the bottom of the garden was still there. He had to cross the lawn first, open the gate and from there walk onto a narrow dirt footpath which ran down to a crossing point across the river. The ten large rocks across the river were still there and as he did before, he would make a jump from one to the other and then take the path which led him to the mine.

Things were going well, and Tony was already working on the mine for a year when one sunny morning, he had just taken a sip of his coffee, the phone rang. It was his eldest brother, and he was terribly upset. "Hallo Tony, this is Michael, I have sad news for you." "Hello Michael, long time no hear. What is going on?" "Mum has taken ill, and things do not look too good for her. I think you should come over to the UK before it is too late." Tony was quite taken aback with this sad news and said he would arrange to fly to London the following day for himself and Sally. He then added, "I would be grateful if someone could pick us up at London Heathrow." Michael agreed to do so. Tony now had to let Sally know immediately so that she could arrange for things during their absence.

Tony was pleased to see his mother and the rest of UK family again and to talk about old times. He was also happy to introduce Sally for the first time. It was sad that their stay in the UK would be limited but Tony knew he needed to get back to continue running the mine.

Whilst there, during a lengthy conversation with his brother, Michael said to him, "It is a shame you did not stay on in the UK, you would have done well for yourself. There was so much going for you here."

Without any hesitation, Tony replied, "I have made a good life in South Africa and thanks to me going to Rhodesia first, I met my wife Sally, and we are doing well. We had three lovely children but, as you are aware we lost our eldest son, Angus, in the Rhodesian war."

Time flew by, it was time for Tony and Sally to return home. They had been three weeks in the UK, enjoyed every minute of their stay but were looking forward to getting back home to the River Bend mine. The day came for their departure, they said their goodbyes to the family and left for South Africa from London Heathrow.

Disaster at River Bend Mine

After the long flight they arrived back in the early morning at Johannesburg's Jan Smuts airport, quite exhausted but happy to touch home ground again. They eventually made their way to the baggage area. Whilst waiting, Tony looked around when he unexpectedly saw a familiar face on the other side of the glass window at "Arrivals." He thought, "what on earth is Vernon doing here at the airport?" They had quite a wait for their baggage. Tony was getting a little nervous wondering what might be awaiting him. Eventually they passed through Customs and met Vernon walking forward to greet them both. As it was Vernon who had originally secured Tony the job at the River Bend mine, he had thought it appropriate for him to pick them up and explain the reason he was at the airport. Tony suddenly got anxious and said, "Vernon, this is a surprise, how nice of you to pick us up. I did not think I was that important to the company." Vernon shook his head and told Tony that he was there because Tony was urgently needed back at the mine. He said, "there has been an accident, it happened yesterday, and the men are working hard to get six miners out of the underground, before the rest of the shaft caves in." Vernon added that they had terrible weather over the past two weeks. It had not stopped raining and that resulted in a part of the tunnel caving in. "Tony," said Vernon, "I don't like to tell you this, but one of the miners is Laura's husband, Jeff Stofberg."

They immediately left the airport and after a few hours of driving they reached the River Bend mine and could see some action going on in the distance. They dropped Sally off at the house and then Tony and Vernon continued to the mine. The scene was lit up by the main flood lights. Many rescuers, miners, first aid people and others including the press correspondent from the local newspaper plus others milling around were there. He saw Laura from the corner of his eye and could see that her hands were covering a part of her face and that her eyes were full of tears. Tony immediately jumped out of the car, ran over to her, and assured her that he would do his best to get Jeff out of the mine alive.

The press turned to Vernon as he was already aware of the situation. "Mr Irvin-Brown," asked one of the journalists, "what can you tell us about this accident?" "Well," said Vernon, "we believe a cable failed, and this caused the elevator to drop down sixty-four feet. We managed to get five miners out, but when we sent the elevator back down, it got stuck to the wall at an angle, so there was no way we could get the last miner out. The miner trapped down there is Jeff Stofberg, one of our top men. He was too far back in the tunnel, and he could not make it to the elevator with the others in time. As we have had a lot of rain, a part of the tunnel has caved in, so this has not helped much. We have now asked a good friend, Johnny, who is from a nearby gold mine, to come over with his crane 'Big Ben' to help get Jeff out of this terrible situation." The reporter thanked Vernon for the update and walked over to some of the miners.

In the meantime, there was worry that there could be an explosion down in the mine, this would make the rescue attempt even more difficult and affect Jeff Stofberg's health.

Time was of the essence, so Johnny enlisted some of the miners to set up the crane. They realised the need to work efficiently and fast to ensure no further calamities would jeopardise the whole operation. After a brief discussion, they determined the best solution was to weld hoops to the top of the elevator, close to the edge and on the side which was wedged into the elevator shaft wall. The rescuers would shackle the two steel wire cables to the elevator to stabilise it. Once done, Johnny would, with the help of the crane, jiggle the elevator loose permitting the operator to lift the elevator clear of the obstruction. The operators then had the choice of trying to lower the elevator or failing that, hauling Jeff out through the cleared space by means of Johnny's crane. Hopefully no additional complications would occur.

The rescue effort continued throughout the night and despite working in shifts, all were exhausted. The next morning one could see the sun rise on the horizon. This signified no rain which gave more hope of getting Jeff up and out of the tunnel without further trouble, freeing him from his two-day entrapment.

Laura had not moved from the spot, her eyes were red from crying, but when she saw Johnny, she called over to him, "how is your 'Big Ben' of a crane performing in the rescue of my husband?" Johnny was taken aback because he did not know that it was his friend Jeff Stofberg who was down below. He half smiled and replied, "operations are going well," and that he would do his utmost to get Jeff out. It was also in his professional interest as a friend and miner to do so.

The moment came when the crane pulled up the elevator freeing the way for Jeff Stofberg's rescue which was completed in the hour. Jeff was slightly bruised but was in good health. Laura could not hold back her tears when she saw Jeff. She ran and put her arms around him. Surprisingly, Jeff's eyes were also filled with tears. It had been touch and go at one point whether they would see one another again. It was such a special moment. Tony and Vernon were also glad to see Jeff and informed him that they would contact him the following day once he had gone through his medical check, to see that everything was well with him.

As they were standing there a truck came up and Johnny said, "that's the new manager of the gold mine where I am working." The manager got out of the truck and walked towards them. Johnny then said, "do you know this guy?" Tony said he did not know him, however, as he got closer, Vernon realised it was his godfather, Richard, whom he had not seen for many years. This was a big surprise to them both. Vernon then explained to the group of men that he had been born in South Africa and that his father and Richard were close friends in the early days. At some time, Vernon's parents went to live in the UK and that is where he spent most of his childhood.

It was time to leave, and Tony suggested to Vernon that it had been a long day and he should stay at his house the night so they could have an early start the next morning to discuss the mine disaster. Tony also asked Richard to join them the next day at 10:30 a.m. "I am sure you can help us with some of our problems." Richard thanked Tony and made his way back to his truck. Vernon turned around to Tony and agreed that it was time to call it a day.

Tony did not sleep very well that night. Thoughts about the mine were going through his head. At 5:00 a.m., the birds were singing to the rising sun. He thought to himself that it would be an eventful day and that he and Vernon needed to get to the bottom of this disaster.

Sally was already making breakfast when Vernon came into the kitchen. He too looked as though he had not had much sleep.

At the arranged time they all met in Tony's office. Once they got settled at the conference table, Tony asked Richard, "how many times a week or month should the elevators and cables be checked and serviced?" Richard said that they need to be checked and serviced at least twice a week. The elevator and cables only had a guarantee of about two years. Both Tony and Vernon raised their eyebrows. Tony then answered, "it seems my foreman and his two assistants have been lying to me all along. I happened to hear through the grapevine that they only did the check once a month. This is fatal to my miners." This was not acceptable as they had not done their job properly. After much discussion they decided to end the meeting. Before leaving, Vernon and Richard agreed to meet up again in Johannesburg once things were cleared up at the River Bend mine.

Due to what was revealed at the previous day's meeting, Tony decided to immediately dismiss the foreman and his two assistants to avoid risks with his miners' lives. The decision was not easy for Tony, he had had a lot of faith in the three guys, but they had made a big mistake to ignore the inspection of the elevator and its cables as per the Mines Rules and Regulations. He knew their absence would make life difficult for a while, but he intended to replace them without delay.

It is now a year later, the mine is doing well, and Tony and Sally are enjoying life. Their two children had graduated and are now working in the UK.

One evening, after dinner, Tony and Sally sat down to a well-earned cup of tea. Tony's thoughts got the better of him and he started to think back at the good old days in the UK and the time he met Vernon before making a life first in Rhodesia and later in South Africa. His thoughts were suddenly jolted by hearing Sally's voice. "Tony, do you want another cup of tea?" "No thank you, Sally, I was just thinking, we could retire in the UK now that the children are settled and working over there. What do you think?" Although Sally had never lived in the UK, she agreed it might be a good decision for their future.

A few weeks later, and after much discussion, Tony decided to give Vernon a call. "Good afternoon, Vernon, hope all is well with you? Sally and I have some news. We have decided to pick up sticks and retire to the UK. I now have the difficult task to let you know that we will be leaving in three months' time. I just wanted to let you know before I hand in my notice." Vernon did not seem to be surprised but understood life in Africa was not so rosy at the present time. Vernon too had a surprise for Tony, and he said, "Tony, believe it or not, but I too am going back to live in the UK. Hopefully, we might live close enough so that we can visit occasionally."

The few months left went by quickly, and it was time for Tony and Sally to say their farewells. They decided to have a farewell party with their friends Vernon Irvin-Brown, Jeff and Laura Stofberg, Pete Smit, not forgetting Richard, Johnny, and Tony's new foreman.

The day came for their departure. Vernon arrived to take them to the airport. It was a long drive and then a long flight, but they knew they were leaving the country with wonderful memories of the past, but also going to another country where they knew their family would be complete again and that this would be another new chapter in their lives.

Happy End

The flight was uneventful but nevertheless enjoyable and relaxing. Tony and Sally had time to reflect on their past, the fun, the successes, and their friends. They had experienced so much action and diversity in their lives that they were positive that whatever confronted them in the future they would have the capability to manage it.

On landing, they sorted out their luggage, made their way through Customs and proceeded to the meeting area. Michael, Tony's brother, was waiting patiently. They were going to stay with him and his family until they reoriented themselves. Their first priority was house selection and once that was accomplished, they would visit other members of the family.

The weather was looking good, and Michael had arranged a "welcome" BBQ for them and the whole family for the following Sunday. The week quickly flew, and Sunday was soon there and to their surprise, so were their own children and their partners. Everyone pitched in and soon the party was underway.

It was so good to see the children, their partners whom they had yet to meet for the first time, and to catch up on what they had been doing since they last touched base. Alice had moved to a new address, but Craig had stayed on in the same village. Tony and Sally arranged to meet up with them again as soon as they had a car, which would be soon because they required a vehicle to ease their search for their own accommodation.

Time went by, Tony and Sally bought a second-hand Station Wagon and after a few trips became more comfortable in their new environment. With their Estate Agent they had already lined up a few houses in the county of Gloucestershire in south-west England. The agent had researched their property needs and they soon selected a house they could afford from their hard-earned savings. The stone house they selected was an old, converted farmhouse with a substantial amount of land and located in the Cotswold's area. The area reminded them of where they had lived in South Africa and the house was so like the one, they had left behind which they had named "Wonderland."

Soon after their purchase they made some alterations to the house and then moved in with some of their furniture which had recently arrived from South Africa. They had already in mind to convert the property to be a Market Garden growing vegetables that could be sold on the local market. This was a good way to get to know neighbours, their village, and its surroundings. They also thought that sometime in the future they could have a roadside stall on the property to cater to the holiday traffic that passed by in the summer months.

As expected, the garden was well suited to their plans and beginning to look well established. Sally's experience in growing vegetables served her well in her goal to grow their produce in larger quantities.

Almost a year passed when out of the blue, Tony received a phone call from Vernon. "Hi, Tony, how are you and Sally getting along?" "Good and it is wonderful to hear from you Vernon. I was wondering what you are doing these days. We are keeping fine and are enchanted by our lovely house and large garden. We have started a vegetable stall at our local market, and it is thriving." "That's good to hear," said Vernon. Tony asked, "where are you at the present time?" Vernon laughed, "you will never guess. I landed in the UK last week and am staying with some friends until I can move into my house which, believe it or not, is also in the Cotswolds." "Really," said Tony, "tell me, where is the house located?" He could not believe his ears when Vernon responded, "well, from what you tell me of your house, my land must be next door to yours. It was an old poultry farm and since I would like to sell chickens and eggs, I thought that would be the ideal place to set up my business." Tony was most pleased at this news and immediately offered to help his friend when he moved in. An idea flashed across his mind in regard to collaborating with his friend and mused, "we could perhaps make good business together."

Within a few weeks Vernon settled himself in the farm next door and arranged to meet up with Tony and Sally at the Fox and Hounds, a local pub. Both sides thought it delightful that they should now, after many years, live and possibly collaborate in their new business ventures. Once they had ordered their drinks they got down to serious business. Tony explained to Vernon that he and Sally were now much involved in not only selling vegetables but also had a side industry making bottled chutneys and jams from their garden products. Vernon thought that was an excellent idea and went on to say that he was going to sell chickens and eggs plus, when the opportunity arose, other poultry like ducks and turkeys. They further discussed their separate aims before Tony piped up and said, "how about us sharing a stall together, that would make things easier and cheaper for us all during these early days of our businesses." They all agreed.

It took a while before they could harvest some of the vegetables so in the meantime Sally kept things going by making her jams and chutneys for the market. Vernon was already starting to sell his eggs. As the peak harvesting time approached Tony decided to get temporary summer help to harvest the vegetables and pack them in small crates and boxes for selling at the market and some local shops. Two summer students were employed from the local agricultural college. In later years, due to the successful work of these students, Tony made a practice of employing students every summer. Both sides profited from this arrangement.

One summer's day Sally noticed Vernon walking jauntily to the market and thought, "I wonder what Vernon has up his sleeve?" Once the market opened Sally decided to ask Vernon why he was suddenly happy with himself, beaming a big smile to all and sundry. Vernon cleared his throat and said, "I have something to tell you and Tony. I know it has taken a long time, but I have decided to get married." "Oh, and to whom may that be?" asked Sally. Vernon replied, "I'm going to marry Betty, the owner of the local coffee shop." Both Sally and Tony smiled, and Sally said, "now I know why you have been selling a lot of eggs. No doubt for Betty's famous egg sandwiches." They gave out a loud laugh together.

Betty had a son, Peter, from her previous marriage. It was some years since her husband passed away. Peter was studying agriculture and came to help Vernon whenever he could, especially during the holidays. He and Vernon got along well together, and it was his intention to take over the farm in the near future.

Time went on, Tony and Sally were enjoying their new lives in the UK. Alice and Craig with partners in tow would often visit them, sometimes together and at other times alone. Vernon and his wife, Betty, were enjoying married life and often joined these family occasions.

It was a lovely, warm summer evening. Tony had just put down some of the tools he used for his vegetable garden. Sally had gone to visit Betty, so he was alone for the next few hours. He decided he would go and relax in the garden for a while, so he walked over to the house, got himself a nice, cold beer and went and sat in the sitting area where Sally had taken a lot of time and patience to plant some flowers and shrubs.

It did not take long before Tony's mind started to drift into the past. He started to think back on his early life in the UK when he was in the army, also when he met Vernon before immigrating to Rhodesia. He started to think of his new working life and how he met his wife, Sally, and the problems they went through together. The birth of his three children and the happiness they brought him. Their life in South Africa and the difficult times they had at the mine. His good friend Vernon who was always there to help when needed. He then started to think again of his eldest son Angus who had been killed by a terrorist during the Rhodesian war. He thought to himself, "I wonder how life would have been had Angus still been here, would we have come to the UK?"

He was suddenly awakened by the noise of a car. He pulled himself together and noticed it was Vernon coming down the pathway in his old Ford truck. Sitting beside him was Sally, he must have decided to give her a lift home. He took another sip of his beer and slowly got up. As Vernon got closer, he shouted out to him, "Vernon, come and join me in a beer." Vernon put up his hand and thanked Tony. Once they got themselves settled, Tony started to tell Vernon of what he had been dreaming about, also the good and bad times they had together in South Africa. Tony then went on to say, "I know that I still miss Angus deeply and I would have loved to have had him here sharing our new life. That, more than anything else, would have given me more fulfilment than having risked our futures by having sought and achieved 'revenge' for his death."

After a few hours passed, Vernon stood up and said he had to go as Betty would be wondering where he had got to. Tony then got up and took Vernon's hand and thanked him for being a good friend and being there for him when he needed someone to talk to.

Vernon got into his truck and called out to Tony, "you take care of yourself, and I'll see you tomorrow at the market."

Tony, feeling better that he had spoken to Vernon about his thoughts, then turned around, went back into the house, and called to Sally, "how about joining me for a night cap?" They sat at the kitchen table and discussed late into the evening what they had done that day. Tony and Sally smiled at one another; they knew that they had done the right thing to start a new life with their family in the UK.